For Fergus Robert

First published 1986 by Walker Books Ltd,
87 Vauxhall Walk, London SE11 5HJ

This edition published 2000

2 4 6 8 10 9 7 5 3 1

© 1986 Shirley Hughes

This book has been typeset in Vendome.

Printed in Hong Kong

British Library Cataloguing in Publication Data
A catalogue record for this book is
available from the British Library.

ISBN 0-7445-6738-6 (hb)
ISBN 0-7445-6984-2 (pb)

Two Shoes, New Shoes

Shirley Hughes

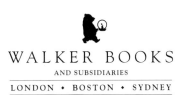

WALKER BOOKS
AND SUBSIDIARIES
LONDON • BOSTON • SYDNEY

Two shoes, new shoes,
Bright shiny blue shoes.

High-heeled ladies' shoes,
For standing tall,

Button-up baby's shoes,
Soft and small.

Slippers, warm by the fire,

Lace-ups in the street.

Gloves are for hands

And socks are for feet.

A crown in a cracker,

A hat with a feather,

Sun hats,

Fun hats,

Hats for bad weather.

A clean white T-shirt laid on the bed,

Two holes for arms ...

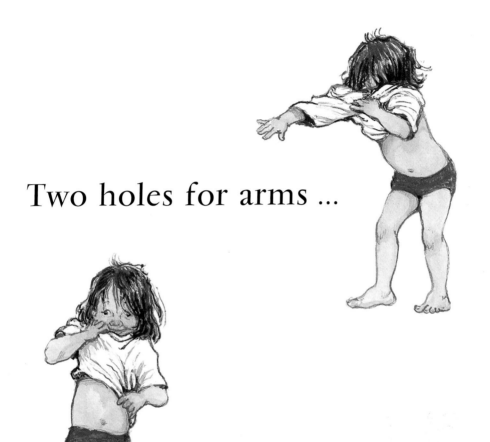

And one for the head.

Zip up a zipper, button a coat,

A shoe for a bed, a hat for a boat.

Wearing it short ...

And wearing it long,

Getting it right ...

And getting it wrong.

Trailing finery,

Dressed for a ball,

And into the bath
Wearing nothing at all!